REDS UNITED!

D. REDMOND

Illustrated by Peter Kavanagh

YOUNG CORGI BOOKS

REDS UNITED!
A YOUNG CORGI BOOK: 0 552 545619

First publication in Great Britain

PRINTING HISTORY
Young Corgi edition published 1998

Set in 16/20pt Bembo Schoolbook
by Phoenix Typesetting Ilkley, West Yorkshire

Young Corgi Books are published by Transworld Publishers Ltd,
61-63 Uxbridge Road, Ealing, London W5 5SA,
in Australia by Transworld Publishers (Australia) Pty. Ltd,
15-25 Helles Avenue, Moorebank, NSW 2170,
and in New Zealand by Transworld Publishers (NZ) Ltd,
3 William Pickering Drive, Albany, Auckland.

Made and printed in Great Britain by
Cox & Wyman Ltd, Reading, Berks.

Suddenly we were playing with a bit of a swagger. On a united front we moved forward and set up a lovely goal-scoring opportunity for Nicky. His shot looked more than hopeful until it bounced off the post. With Gransden's frustration clearly mounting, we broke through their scattered defence again and Xin, one on one with the goalie, trickled the ball around him and WHAM!

We were on top. 2–1. It was almost too good to be true!

Don't miss any of the titles in
this great football series:

COME ON, YOU REDS!
PENALTY!
UP FOR THE CUP!
REDS UNITED!

For Colleen and Luke,
with love - DR

For Paddy, who has
always supported the Reds!
with love - PK

Joe   Angus   Maureen   Eddie

Usha   Domino   Xin   Rocco

Leo   Luke   Nicky   Al

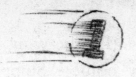

I'm Rocco Angelo, midfielder for Prickwillow United, and right now I have only TWO thoughts in my head – the Inter-schools Cup semi-final and the Inter-schools Cup final! Luckily my best mate, Luke, and all the rest of Prickwillow United have exactly the same two thoughts in their heads, so I'm not the only thinking man in the team!

Flipperbottom, our brilliant football coach and class teacher, tried to start the summer term with a firm warning.

(By the way, his *real* name is Shipperbottom but we changed it to Flipperbottom because his bum sticks out when he jogs! Fair enough, really.)

"Your exams are this term," Flipperbottom reminded us on the first day of term. "So, it's work first and football later."

It was a case of in one ear and out the other with us lot. Football second? Dream on! I tried my best in class, though to be honest my best had never really been good enough when it came to schoolwork – and that was even before I became a football fanatic!

"So when do we find out who we're playing in the semis?" asked Eddie.

"Depends on the draw," Flipperbottom replied with a tantalizing smile.

"We should know soon," Nicky, our talented winger reasoned. "We're playing the semis a week on Friday."

"Two weeks!" I gulped. "We need *much* more practice and we haven't even got a league game this week. Sir, couldn't you arrange a friendly for us?"

"St Olaf's phoned to say they'd be keen on another friendly game," he replied.

"Not them again," groaned Luke, whose cousin James went to St Olaf's, a posh local private school.

"They're a nice enough bunch," Flipperbottom reminded him.

"Not if you've got the cousin from hell playing in defence," Luke muttered moodily.

"They do a nice tea at St Olaf's," Maureen McGuinness chimed up. "Remember all those cucumber sandwiches and chocolate eclairs we got last time?"

"And the pitch is the best we've ever played on," Angus said. "Soft and green as velvet," he added, suddenly going poetic.

We all nodded. St Olaf's did have its advantages. Anyway, who were Prickwillow United to find fault? We were still playing league football in red P.E. kits and our pitch was a joke!

"Glad you approve," joked Flipperbottom, "because the game's fixed for tomorrow at four thirty. Tell your parents," he added firmly. "I don't want anybody earwigging me for neglecting my duties."

"How many more practice sessions have we got before the semis?" I asked.

"Three, if we're lucky," Flipperbottom replied.

"That's cutting it fine, sir," I fretted.

"Roc, get real," Flipperbottom chuckled. "When have we *ever* done anything otherwise?"

As the chief worrier and nail-biter in the team I called an emergency meeting that night on the village recreational ground.

"What is it this time, Roc?" Xin asked, clearly fed up with me but trying hard to be patient.

"I'm worried," I blurted out.

"So, what's new?' giggled Nicky. "There are two things you're good at, Roc: playing in midfield, and worrying."

"Somebody has to worry," I retorted hotly. "Here we are on the verge of history," I said, suddenly remembering an expression I'd heard on the telly the night before.

12

"Verge of history my foot!" scoffed Al.

"We are!" said Leo, taking my side. "This time last year Prickwillow United didn't even exist. Now we're one of the main contenders for the Inter-schools Cup."

"RIGHT!" I said, glad that somebody was backing me.

"You only arrived last term, Al," Maureen McGuinness pointed out. "You've no idea what this school was like before Flipperbottom showed up and formed the football team."

"Grim, I should think," said Al.

We all nodded our heads.

"Dead grim," said Luke.

"What's up, Roc?" asked Usha briskly. "You've not dragged us all out tonight just to share your worries."

"I think we've got to increase our practice sessions," I replied. "Play as much as we can – both in and out of school."

"Easy," said Nicky, springing to his feet. "Just pass us the ball!"

Without a moment's hesitation we fell into our positions. Joe, the biggest and the tallest, was in goal. Maureen McGuinness led the defence with

14

Angus, Usha and Eddie. I was in midfield with Xin, Al and Leo. Luke and Nicky were out on the wings. My nerves fell away as we moved up and down the pitch, confident and familiar with each other's strengths and weaknesses. Joe was unbeatable in goal, like a rock! Our defence was fast and fluid. Al and Leo were superb at sweeping long balls out to the flanks and Xin was spectacular at losing her marker. Luke was magic at darting runs and Nicky Chang could get around *anybody*! Me? Rocco Angelo. Well I was sort of good at everything!

15

After about half an hour we all flopped down on the grass, hot and gasping for breath. Suddenly chimes rang out across the rec, combined with the smell of frying fish.

"It's Mum!" cried Nicky, running towards the mobile chippy that was parked up by the rec.

"Hi!" called cheery Mrs Chang as she opened her shop window and waved to us all. "Fancy a bag of chips?"

"YEAH!" we yelled as we mobbed her van.

In between handing out bags of steaming hot chips Mrs Chang said, "I've just met the headmaster of Gamlingay School."

We all stopped what we were doing, momentarily frozen in time. Gamlingay School was one of the final four in the semis.

"Yes . . . ?" said Nicky with the vinegar bottle poised in mid-air.

"They're doing the draw tomorrow," she said.

"Oh . . ." We all let out a groan of disappointment.

"I thought you were going to tell us who we were playing," grumbled Nicky.

"You'll know soon enough," she said in her best no-nonsense voice. "Now finish your chips and don't be late home!"

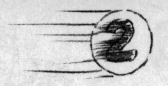

St Olaf's was as posh as we remembered: immaculate grounds, a winding drive and a pitch to die for!

"WOW!" gasped Al, who hadn't been with us on the first visit.

"Wait till you see the tea," whispered Maureen McGuinness.

It was impossible to believe there was SO much free food on offer – cucumber sandwiches, crisps, warm sausage rolls and four kinds of cream cake. Before a normal league game I'd never have eaten a thing, but knowing that this was a friendly made us all very laid back.

We stuffed our faces and when the kick-off whistle blew we were like a squad of dumplings on the move! Almost immediately St Olaf's slid in a goal which at least three of us should have stopped. Seeing the ball moving towards the net was like the kind of nightmare where you're being chased by a monster but your legs won't move. That was me with a full and overloaded belly!

"MOVE!" bellowed Flipperbottom who was watching goggle-eyed from the sideline.

"I would if I could," I thought desperately.

"Should've laid off the cream cakes," smirked James as he flashed by.

"We've been set up," I thought as I darted down the pitch after him. "Stuffed on cream cakes!"

Suddenly I understood the meaning of 'bust a gut' as I sprinted after St Olaf's attack, determined to get the ball out from under them. With cramping pains darting through my stomach, I lunged and intercepted the ball and booted it back down the field.

Good old Nicky picked it up and, though he didn't do much with it, he made St Olaf's sweat a little.

Throughout the whole of the first half poor Joe in the goal area was being bombarded with volleys, headers and lobs. Without his strength and skill we could easily have finished that first half five down instead of only one.

At half-time I turned down my orange juice and set to on some *serious* exercises.

"Roc! Shouldn't you be formulating some attacking moves for the second half instead of doing press-ups?" snapped Flipperbottom.

"I am," I gasped. "St Olaf's set us up for losers when they dished out the cream cakes."

"That's right," Maureen agreed. "I've been feeling queasy since we kicked off."

"Burn it off!" I urged the team. "Or they'll slaughter us!"

We came out a trimmer and more determined team. As the second half whistle went we were after that ball like greyhounds out of the slips! We closed down the opposition before they could blink, tackled strongly and played the ball forward quickly. All we needed now was goals.

"Yes, yes!" I muttered to myself as I saw the goal area opening up before me at last.

With a storming header I aimed at that tantalizing space but only managed to rattle the bar. "NO!" I groaned through gritted teeth.

But fortunately Al ran on to the bouncing ball and chested it in before the goalie could recover himself.

One—all. Then just before the final whistle, the game ended with a superb volley from Xin that put us 2—1 up.

"Thanks for a great game," I said as, captain to captain, James and I shook hands. "And for the tea!"

On the way home our school bus drew up at the same lights as Mrs Chang's mobile chippy.

"Who won?" she asked, eagerly leaning out of the window.

"We did!" called Nicky.

"That's good," she answered, with a wide grin, "because I've just heard the results of the draw."

"Who are we playing?" we all yelled together.

"Gransden Rovers," she replied. Then the lights turned green and she drove off.

"How come your mum knows more about the fixtures than me?" Flipperbottom asked Nicky.

"You can't keep a secret from my mum," laughed Nicky. "She knows the latest gossip before it's even happened!"

Rumours about Gransden Rovers flew around Prickwillow that weekend faster than a Harrier jump-jet! Luke and I talked to some local lads who'd played them and they told us stories that made our hair stand on end.

"Determined," one said.

"Brought one of our attackers down and broke his arm," the other added grimly.

Luke went white and I felt sick.

"Blimey!' I gasped.

"For an encore they broke the goalie's nose," the first boy continued. "Not on purpose, of course. They just kicked it instead of the ball!"

Later that afternoon we saw Al.

"Heard about Gransden Rovers?" he asked.

"I've heard too much and it's all bad," I replied.

"Well, get this," said Al. "They got through the quarter-finals with only ten men."

"They sound superhuman," I groaned.

"Superhuman and well hard!" he added grimly.

By Monday morning we were all stressed out and Flipperbottom had a serious job trying to calm us down.

"Get a grip!" he said in his loudest, firmest voice.

"But Gransden are legend, sir," I blurted out.

"And so are we," he replied in a tone that commanded respect. "Prickwillow United have come from nowhere in seven short months. That didn't happen by accident. It was *destiny*," he said, his eyes blazing with conviction. "We've worked hard, pushed ourselves and never once thought we couldn't face our opponents. We're superb — just believe it!"

There was a stunned silence. We'd never heard Flipperbottom speak so proudly of us before

"Wow!" I gasped. "Do you really think we're THAT good?"

Flipperbottom beamed and hit his palm hard against mine. "The best, Roc. Simply the best!"

We had a practice session on Monday after school and one on Thursday, the eve of the semis. Flipperbottom concentrated hard on our tackles.

"Go in attacking and keep it that way," he urged. "They're expecting a walkover so knock their socks off the minute you run on. Surprise is the element of the game," he concluded with a wink.

An unexpected surprise came our way during the final practice session when Joe, in goal, overstretched himself and knocked back the index finger on his right hand.

"AHHH!" he bellowed, hopping about in agony. "Ouch! OOH! It hurts."

Flipperbottom managed to calm him down enough to look at the finger. It was swelling up like a black pudding!

"Blimey, Joe. Why weren't you wearing your gloves?"

"I left them at home," Joe confessed.

"That's going to be a whopper!" said Flipperbottom anxiously. "I'd better get you down to Casualty for an X-ray."

Five minutes later he was driving out of the school gates with Joe in the passenger seat looking really hacked off. We all slumped gloomily back out on to the pitch.

"What if Joe can't play tomorrow?" Eddie muttered.

In the heavy silence that followed, Luke pointed out the blindingly obvious. "We haven't got a reserve."

"Well there's no way we can play without a goalie!" Maureen McGuinness cried. "I mean, that'd be daft!"

Nobody could argue with that!

"So, we'll have ten men when we face Gransden," I said in a voice that sounded like it came from the grave. "TEN MEN," I said, piling on the agony. "For a semi-final game!"

"Better try out some goalies," urged Leo, "just in case Joe really is laid up."

One by one we took a turn in goal and I can tell you we were *hopeless*.

"I never knew it was THIS hard," grumbled Angus as the ball bounced off his head and into the net.

"No blinking wonder Joe bent his finger back," cried Xin. "My hands are killing me."

Maureen had the bulk to go in goal but was as nimble as a tank on the move. Xin was agile but built like a flea! Nicky and Luke were both good but we couldn't afford to take them off the wings.

"It's got to be somebody from the midfield or defence," said Xin firmly. After eliminating everybody else, the final choice fell between me and Eddie.

"Let's spin for it," I said.

As Angus flicked a penny I prayed I'd lose. No way did I want to be in goal during the semi-finals. I wanted to be captain, in midfield! Unfortunately the penny fell face down.

"You lose, Roc," said Angus.

My heart sank like a brick but I tried to put a cheerful face on an already grim situation. "No worries," I said.

 Two hours later, back home, I had a phone call from Flipperbottom. "How's Joe?" I asked.

"His finger's not broken but it's badly swollen," he replied. "I hear you're in goal if Joe doesn't make the semis game."

"That's right," I answered.

"Excellent," Flipperbottom said. "I've done a bit of swopping around and put Luke in as captain. Sorry I couldn't tell you earlier but I was a bit preoccupied with dashing off to hospital with Joe."

33

Even when the receiver went dead I still stood there with the phone pressed to my ear. I wasn't the captain any more, I wasn't playing in midfield and we were going out to play a legendary team with ME in goal!

I had very little sleep that night and when I got to school I had rings under my eyes as big as fried eggs. Instead of running up to join me in the playground Luke hung back, awkward and self-conscious.

"Sorry, mate," he mumbled.

I shrugged and tried hard to sound like I didn't care.

34

"It's cool," I said. "Flipperbottom's always changing the captain."

Luke knew me too well for that kind of rubbish. "Roc!" he cried. "Come off it. You're pig-sick about his decision, and I'm not exactly over the moon. You're my best mate."

"You're right. I am totally cheesed off about everything! TEN MEN and me in goal!" I blurted out. "We don't need a captain, we need a miracle!"

Luke giggled and thumped me hard on the back. "I'll do my best, mate, but I'm making no promises!"

We were away to Gransden and you've never seen a quieter football team than Prickwillow United on their way to face their opponents.

"Cheer up, you lot," urged Flipperbottom from the driving seat of the minibus. "It's not a funeral."

"It could be," I muttered under my breath.

As we stepped off the bus, two good things happened simultaneously. The sun popped out from behind a bank of grey clouds and Joe hopped out of his mum's car.

"I'm playing!" he yelled as he fisted the air, his injured hand cocooned in a huge goalie glove.

"That should be handy for shovelling out the goals," I joked as I poked his glove.

"Just what I thought," chuckled Joe.

Flipperbottom gave Joe a bear-hug.
"Good on you lad!" he said. "Rocco,
you're back in midfield."

"Brilliant!" I yelled.

It was great to run on, a whole team
with a sound goalie, though I felt
uncomfortable when the team looked
to me for guidance.

"Luke's captain," I whispered as I ran
down the pitch with Maureen and Al
flanking me.

"But he's not leading us," Maureen
said. "We need direction."

37

I didn't dare say anything to Luke. He'd got enough on his plate dodging an opponent half the size of a house! Luke was my best mate, my main man. I didn't want to do anything wrong by him. However, as the minutes ticked away, it became clear that we did have a problem of leadership. It was the sort of problem you couldn't afford to have in a cup semi-final so I reluctantly took the law into my own hands.

"Keep it up, keep it up!" I shouted as we pushed forward.

Hearing my words Luke turned around and I winked hard. "Good work," he said, instantly getting the message. "Keep it up," he cried, echoing my words.

Gransden seemed determined to take us apart but we weathered their early onslaught with surprising skill. Al astonished his opponent with a high jump that sent a header arrowing towards the goal. Unfortunately it was flashed over but it showed Gransden that we were no pushover! As half-time neared our energy levels sank along with our concentration. Sensing a kill, Gransden pounced. One of their big wingers chested a ball through most of our defence and they took the lead seconds before the whistle went.

There was an awkwardness in the changing room at half-time.

"Say something," I whispered to Luke. He didn't have a clue!

"Anybody want an orange?" he asked.

"Something constructive," I squeaked in a tiny, indignant voice. "You're the captain!"

The penny finally dropped. "We've done brilliantly," said Luke boldly. "And we're going to get through," he added, as he punched the air.

The team nodded and smiled appreciatively.

"Blimey, it's hard thinking for ten players," grumbled Luke as we ran back on.

"Keep their spirits up," I advised. "It's a tough game and we need YOUR leadership."

Luke gulped. "Heck, Roc! You're so much better at this than me."

We immediately set the tone for a dramatic second half with a thrilling end-to-end exchange that stunned the opposition. A lovely long ball from Eddie led to Angus who crossed the ball to Luke. Luke volleyed the ball under the bar and into the roof of the

net. We were now level pegging with Gransden. One apiece and all of us feverishly overexcited!

The team needed calming down and it was the captain's job to do it.

"Stay cool," I heard myself saying. "Keep on the ball. Don't waste chances."

Luke gave me a thumbs-up, clearly grateful for all the help he could get.

What with worrying about Luke and the rest of my team-mates, I hadn't even noticed that Gransden were suddenly beginning to flake at the edges. Luckily Flipperbottom had.

"Keep up the attack!" he yelled from the sideline.

Suddenly we were playing with a bit of a swagger. On a united front we moved forward and set up a lovely goal-scoring opportunity for Nicky. His shot looked more than hopeful until it bounced off the post. With Gransden's frustration clearly mounting, we broke through their scattered defence again and Xin, one on one with the goalie, trickled the ball around him and WHAM!

We were on top. 2–1. It was almost too good to be true!

"Don't take any chances!" I bellowed as we regrouped.

"Stay calm!" Luke added.

Gransden came back with a vengeance but their determination fizzled into a froth of messy balls and reckless tackles that suddenly made me nervous. The hairs on the back of my neck prickled as I sensed danger.

"Be careful!" I yelled.

Hardly were the words out of my mouth when Al tripped over his tenacious opponent and fell full length, cutting his chin open as he landed. Like a hero he tried to play on but the blood was gushing fast and furious.

Flipperbottom helped Al off and we were down to ten players for the last few minutes of injury time.

Gransden now threw everything but the kitchen sink at us. They stormed the goal area and a lesser man than Joe would have run for cover. When they powered a mighty driving header at him, bang on target, he flung himself wide and superbly flipped the ball out to Maureen.

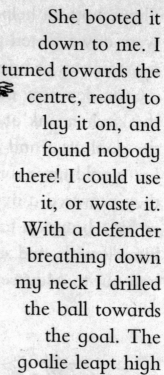

She booted it down to me. I turned towards the centre, ready to lay it on, and found nobody there! I could use it, or waste it. With a defender breathing down my neck I drilled the ball towards the goal. The goalie leapt high to intercept the shot and slipped. As he crash-landed, the ball nestled cosily in the back of the net. 3–1. In a daze I saw Flipperbottom dancing up and down, singing at the top of his voice. "Nothing's going to stop us, nothing's going to stop us!"

"Nothing's going to stop us now!" we all shouted together.

Al's dad, arriving to take him off to Casualty, sobered us up briefly, but the minute we got in the school bus we sang ourselves hoarse.

"Glory, glory, Reds United! Glory, glory, Reds United!"

"Hurray!" yelled our friends as we drove into the school playground.

"HURRAY!" cheered Mrs Chang who was parked outside the gates, filling paper bags with hot chips for us all.

"Do you think she'll know who we're playing in the final?" asked Joe excitedly.

"No chance," Flipperbottom replied. "The other semis game is tomorrow and I am personally going to watch it."

"Checking out the competition, sir?" teased Nicky.

"Just call it a bit of market research," Flipperbottom replied with a wink.

On Monday Flipperbottom announced our opponents in the Cup Final.

"Hatley Lions, at home, this Friday afternoon," he said.

"Who are they?" asked Angus.

"Never heard of them," said Leo.

"They're a new team, like us, who've come from nowhere and stormed their way through the season," Flipperbottom explained.

"How did they play on Saturday?" I asked.

"They're good," Flipperbottom said. "Fast, inventive and they work really well together."

"Terrific," I grumbled.

"What do you want me to say?" Flipperbottom laughed. "They were hopeless? Get real, Roc. This is the Cup Final. The opposition is going to be good. *Really* good!"

"All right, sir," I said. "Stop laying it on with a trowel!"

"At least we're playing at home," said Xin. "We should pull a good crowd."

"Who's going to be captain?" asked Luke in a voice that said, *please* don't let it be me!

"Rocco," said Flipperbottom without a moment's hesitation.

"Phew! That's a relief," laughed Luke.

We practised like crazy all week, whether it was an arranged practice at school, or just a knockabout on the rec.

"Just keep on playing," Flipperbottom urged. "Eat, drink and sleep football, until you're even playing it in your sleep."

By the end of the week we were as fit as butchers' dogs and I for one was *sleepwalking* football! Mum found me on the landing, in my pyjamas, trying to whack an imaginary ball across the landing and down the stairs!

"Gotta get an equalizer," I mumbled as she steered me back into bed. "You will, love, you will," she soothed as she pulled the duvet around me.

It was only after the last practice session that Eddie had the foresight to mention that we hadn't got any reserves! You'd think after the stress of the semis game, playing with only ten in the closing minutes of the match, that we'd be on the ball about reserves for the final.

Fortunately Xin had a brainwave. "Let's ask Ayan and Domino, for old times' sake," she suggested.

We all nodded. Both of them had helped set up Prickwillow United at the start of the season and both had been forced to withdraw from the team due to circumstances beyond their control.

"Cool!" I said. "I'll ask them now!"

Both lads agreed to join the squad and running on with them for that momentous Cup Final was a real joy. Together we'd all made history and this was the day when fate decided whether we went down in the history books or were just remembered as a brief but glorious flash in the pan.

"HURRAY!" cheered our supporters. "HURRAY!" Strong hands thumped our backs and patted our shoulders as we made our way out.

"You can do it, lad," smiled my mum, with tears in her eyes.

"You're the BEST!" beamed Mrs Chang, waving her red and white scarf.

"Go for it," gulped Flipperbottom, who was almost as nervous as we were.

We felt like gladiators as we ran on to the pitch which was gently licked by a breeze that was heaven-sent for lifting the ball. I smiled as we won the toss. Whatever happened I'd remember today for the rest of my life!

When the whistle blew we all knew exactly what Flipperbottom meant about Hatley Lions. They were keen and inventive, hungry and determined – just like us! They'd come from nowhere in a single season and were as hungry for the cup as we were. As we moved into play neither side gave an inch. We ran up and down, both sides presenting a solid wall of concrete resistance. It's hard to sustain that kind of tactic, and pretty boring for the spectators too. Somebody has to give and, luckily for us, Hatley briefly lost their concentration. In their temporary lapse they opened up too many spaces and we saw the goalmouth for the first time since the game had started. It was like a red rag to a bull! Al took a long ball from deep within the midfield, chested it down and swerved it over to Nicky on the wing. He passed it with a neat little chip straight to me on the edge of the area and without pausing to breathe I placed it past the keeper with a simple sidefoot. 1–0 and every red bobble-hat and scarf going sky-high on the sideline.

"YEAH!"

This was a walkover. We're going to take Hatley Lions apart, I thought.

Ten minutes later I was eating my heart out. The opposition came at us like a real pack of lions! Angus handled the ball in the goal area and the Hatley striker scored a superb penalty that left us gobsmacked. It was *us* who were now taking the beating as the opposition motored up and down the pitch, putting a strain on our already depleted energy.

I was praying for the half-time whistle to go before somebody went and did something stupid – then I went and did something *totally* stupid! During a hot and nasty scuffle I sent the ball *exactly* where I didn't want it to go – right over the goal line. From a dangerously low, in-swinging corner, the Hatley winger glanced it past the near post just as the half-time whistle went. I was totally GUTTED!

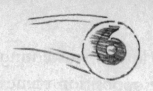

"Hang in there," Flipperbottom urged as we sat, hunched up and dejected, in the changing room. "There's half the game left and only one goal in it."

Half a game, I thought to myself. Maybe I'd score a couple of own goals to round off my first give-away!

We ran on with the Hatley supporters trying their best to drown our lot out, but Prickwillow were having NONE of it!

"Oh, we love you, Prickwillow!" they chanted. "Oh, we love you, we do. Oh, we love you, Prickwillow. Prickwillow – WE LOVE YOU!"

Now, how could you let loyal supporters like that down? A flash of determination went through the team like an electric charge.

"This half's OURS!" I said through gritted teeth.

We instantly took control and produced some pretty confident passes which seemed to set big Maureen McGuinness alight. She suddenly let fly from twenty-five yards with a wonderfully accurate shot that powered the ball over the goalie's grasping fingers and dipped gracefully under the crossbar. Hatley were stunned – and so were we. Less than a minute into the second half and Maureen had equalized with a classic shot!

Upstaged Hatley came back with a driving through ball that would have made it but for a heroic sliding tackle by Angus for which he paid a very high price.

"OWWW!" he howled, locked in cramping agony.

He was helped off by Al's dad and Flipperbottom brought on the subs, taking the opportunity to replace Usha who'd clearly run out of steam. Having Domino and Ayan back in the team was a bit like old times.

"Go for it!" they shouted as they ran on.

Eddie collected the ball and on a long run sent it zipping down the field to Xin who immediately took possession. In a mad rush of enthusiasm Eddie moved forwards leaving a big hole in defence.

"Get back!" I screamed.

Hatley's lanky right back was quicker on the case than Eddie. He sent the ball cracking down the touchline on to the boot of their right winger who headed straight for the penalty box.

"They're going to score!" I gasped.

And they did! 3–2, in the closing quarter, thanks to Eddie's sudden headrush. Seeing Mrs Chang drop her head between her hands said it all. We were in deep, deep trouble. Hatley on the other hand were as high as kites.

"WHO-AH!" they roared as they rolled and tumbled in front of their supporters.

We kicked off with some determined deep runs into opposition territory. Then Xin ran along-side two defenders for fifteen yards before guiding a right-foot shot between them.

Ayan outpaced his opponent to meet it and smashed the ball to Luke. He met the cross and headed it low past the keeper. 3–3!

The final could go down in history as a glorious draw but that just wasn't enough for me. I could just feel goals in the air – OUR GOALS!

"Fight! Fight! Fight!" I shouted.

As the last minutes of the game faded we went into hyperdrive, blocking and thwarting Hatley's every move.

"Just one more," I prayed out loud. "Only one more . . ."

Domino answered my prayer. With breathtaking precision, his left foot made contact with the ball twenty-five yards out and sent it screaming through the defence into the corner of the net. 4–3.

As the whistle went I fell face down on the earth, almost crying with relief.

"We won, we won!" I sobbed in a daze of happiness.

"Buried 'em!" laughed Flipperbottom. "Totally buried 'em!"

Jumping and running, hugging and cheering, we ran up to our supporters and applauded them.

"You're the best!" I shouted over and over again.

Our wild jubilation was interrupted by the appearance of the silver trophy, fluttering with OUR red ribbons!

"Well done, Prickwillow United," said the chairman of the Inter-schools' committee. "You've come far this season and certainly deserve to be the Inter-schools' Cup Final Champions."

I clutched the cup tight, kissed it then raised it high.

"We are the champions!" I shouted.

"YEAH!" went up the loudest roar
I've ever heard in my life.

Holding the cup we did our lap of
honour, singing the song we all loved
best.

"Glory, glory, Reds united.
Glory, glory, Reds united.
Glory, glory, Reds united.
We'll go marching on – on – on!"

THE END